DATE DUE

E
crag
c.1

Gage, Wilson   2322
      A wild goose tale

"Many boys will sympathize with Chuck who
seems to have a great ability to do the wrong
thing at the wrong time. On a camping trip
with his uncle the relationship between boy
and uncle is well portrayed. Pen-and-ink
sketches."   — Library Journal

B 5-174

A WILD GOOSE TALE

A
Wild Goose Tale

STORY BY WILSON GAGE

PICTURES BY GLEN ROUNDS

THE WORLD PUBLISHING COMPANY
CLEVELAND AND NEW YORK

PUBLISHED BY The World Publishing Company
2231 West 110th Street, Cleveland 2, Ohio

PUBLISHED SIMULTANEOUSLY IN CANADA BY
Nelson, Foster & Scott Ltd.

Library of Congress Catalog Card Number: 61-6655

MWP

For my favorite author
William O. Steele

Contents

Chuck

CHUCK was just about to multiply 37 by 46 when Miss Latimore came in and said school was dismissed. He hardly heard what she said, he was so glad not to have to do the problem. He never *could* remember what 6 × 7 was.

He ran all the way home. On the sidewalks the red-and-brown leaves made a pleasant racket as he ran. The October sky was clear and blue. All along the edge of the sky he could see the hazy shapes of the Smoky Mountains.

Mother and Daddy were eating lunch in the kitchen.

"Why, Chuck!" cried Mother. "What's wrong? Are you sick?"

Chuck puffed and panted. "No'm," he answered at last. "But school's out. It's out till next Monday . . . I think she said Monday. Or maybe Tuesday. Or Friday. Or something."

"Well, why?" asked Mother.

Chuck screwed up his face, trying to remember. He should have paid more attention. Measles? Did everybody

9

have the measles? No, that wasn't it. The circus maybe? Had school been let out so everyone could go to the circus? The furnace! That was it, the furnace.

"The furnace has the measles," he told his mother, and grinned. "Honest, Mother, it was the furnace. Something happened to it and they've got to put in a new one."

"Oh, yes," said Mother. "We talked about that at the PTA meeting. I'd forgotten. Oh, dear!"

"What's the matter?" asked Daddy.

"Well, it's just that this is a bad time to have Chuck home," Mother explained. "The men are going to be here papering and painting all this week. And the baby's so cross and fretful since she's had this cold. I've asked Mrs. Harrell to come over and take care of her in the mornings while I'm busy. And you know, Chuck upsets Mrs. Harrell."

Chuck turned red. It wasn't his fault things happened every time Mrs. Harrell came to the house. He certainly hadn't meant to turn his jar of tadpoles over in her lap. Some of them were more than halfway frogs. And that time he'd locked her in the cellar and gone off to play with Johnny Parker—he hadn't even known she was anywhere around, much less down in his basement.

"Nonsense," said Daddy. "Chuck's no trouble. He'll be a help to you, I expect."

Mother didn't say anything. But she still looked worried.

10

"After lunch, I'm going to burn some trash," Daddy told Chuck. "Then I'm going to rake leaves. How about helping me?"

"I guess that'll be okay," said Chuck gloomily. Was he going to have to be a help all the time? He might as well have stayed in school and figured out what 6×7 was.

He even had to eat his school lunch. The ham sandwich was good and the apple was all right, but the hard-boiled egg was pooey. And then when he was almost too full to eat them, Mother gave him three chocolate cookies. He finished his milk with the cookies and went outdoors.

Daddy was burning paper in the incinerator. "Bring the wheelbarrow around here," he told Chuck. "We can use it to carry leaves."

The wheelbarrow was in the front yard where Daddy had been using it in the morning. Chuck liked to push it, though it was heavy and a little hard-to-handle.

He could never explain how it happened. The driveway sloped rather steeply toward the bottom, and the wheelbarrow *was* heavy. It just seemed to get away from him and run of its own accord. It slammed into the incinerator, and the big can turned over, spilling burning papers out on the dry leaves. Sparks flew everywhere and little flames sprang up all over the lawn.

Daddy grabbed a broom and began to beat at the fire. "Get the hose out of the garage, Chuck," he called. "And hurry!"

Chuck picked himself up off the ground where the wheelbarrow had thrown him. He couldn't think what Daddy wanted the hoes for. Was he going to dig a trench around the fire?

But Chuck did as he was told. It was dim in the garage, and the hoes were hard to find. They were way in the back behind the shovels and a lawn chair. One of them got tangled in the legs of the chair. When he stooped to try to get it out, a shovel fell over and hit him in the head.

"Come on!" Daddy yelled. "Hurry, Chuck!"

Chuck rubbed his head, jerked up the hoes, and ran out of the garage. "Here they are, Daddy," he called. "Here they are!"

Daddy didn't say anything. He just dropped his broom and ran past Chuck into the garage. When he came out, he was dragging the coils of the rubber hose. He fastened it to the hydrant and turned it on full force. The leaves were burning merrily, but he soon had the fire out. He sprinkled the leaves well and dampened a big circle all around the place where the grass had caught.

Chuck didn't say anything either. He put the two hoes down and rubbed the knot on his head again. There was a cut on his hand from falling in the driveway. He wiped the blood off with one finger and rubbed it on his blue jeans.

Daddy turned off the water, wound up the hose, and

put it back in the garage. He put back the hoes, too. Then he went into the house. Chuck followed him sadly.

Mother was in the kitchen mixing something in a bowl. "Now what?" she asked.

"Didn't your brother Bill say he was going camping this week?" asked Daddy. "And didn't he say he'd like to take Chuck sometime?"

Mother smiled. "Yes, he did," she answered. "You know, I think that's a pretty good idea!"

Chuck thought his Uncle Bill was the most wonderful person in the world. As they bounced along through the woods in the jeep, Chuck thanked his lucky stars the old furnace had broken down. Getting to go on a camping trip with Uncle Bill was just about the neatest thing he could think of.

The place they were headed for was only about twenty-five miles from home. But it took a good while to get there, for the roads were rough and winding.

When they stopped, it didn't take long to unpack. "I don't have a tidy nature," Uncle Bill explained. "So I don't like to bring much stuff with me. That way I don't have much chance to make a real first-class mess."

"Do you come here often?" Chuck wanted to know.

Uncle Bill lifted another box out of the jeep. "Pretty often in the fall and winter," he replied. "It's the nearest place where I can see waterfowl—ducks and geese, and

14

some shore birds. But I hardly ever come here in the spring and summer. The ducks are gone then, and I know better places to watch heron and such creatures in warm weather.''

"Did you used to come here when you were my age?" asked Chuck.

Uncle Bill shook his head. "No, because the lake wasn't here. It wasn't till the dam was built that the river backed up and spread out into a lake, and then the ducks began to spend the winter here. And the dam was built about fifteen years ago.''

"Is that the lake?" asked Chuck, pointing.

"What did you think it was, a volcano?" answered Uncle Bill. "Here, stack these cans by the stove. I'll get my field glasses and we'll go look."

When they got to the lake, Chuck was thrilled. "Gee, an island," he exclaimed. "Two or three islands. I like islands.''

"I like islands too," said Uncle Bill. "So do the ducks and geese. But somehow geese don't seem to like *these* islands. They come here every now and then, but they never stay."

"What are those things? Are they geese?" asked Chuck, pointing to three little dark objects out on the water.

"No," Uncle Bill answered. "They're grebes. Pied-billed grebes, they're called. Take my field glasses and look at them, and I'll show you something funny."

16

It took a while for Chuck to figure out what to do with the glasses. They were heavy and he kept looking at his shoelaces or the patch on Uncle Bill's jacket instead of the grebes. But at last he got the glasses focused on the birds.

"Now, hold steady," Uncle Bill said. "You just stay here and watch."

He began to walk slowly around the edge of the lake toward the grebes. Chuck watched. He thought surely the birds would fly away or swim off. But they didn't. They just sank lower and lower into the water. Their backs disappeared little by little until only their necks and heads were sticking out. Finally—one, two, three—the heads vanished under the water. Chuck laughed.

"How was that?" Uncle Bill called, coming back toward him.

"Where'd they go?" asked Chuck. "Won't they drown?"

"Nope," said Uncle Bill. "They're fine divers and underwater swimmers. Look, here they come now."

And three tiny birds bobbed up on the water, a long way from the place where the grebes had disappeared.

"Gee, what's that?" Chuck wanted to know, pointing down the beach. "Gosh, it's big. Look at it! It's all ragged in the front."

"It's a great blue heron," Uncle Bill told him. "There's

another one flying over. They're big, all right. I used to know a man who always called them 'Forty-gallons-of-soup.' Come on, maybe we can get a little closer to that one on the ground.''

Chuck and Uncle Bill walked along the edge of the lake, but the big long-legged heron drew in his neck, spread his great wings, and flew.

"Never mind," said Uncle Bill. "The best part of camping here is that there's always something to see. Not just birds either. All kinds of animals live here in these woods.''

And right away Chuck found something he thought was a starfish, but Uncle Bill said it was a water-measuring earthstar.

"Is it an animal?" asked Chuck.

"No," answered Uncle Bill. "It's a fungus, like a mushroom. It starts out as a little round ball. But when it gets damp it opens out into that pretty star shape. That's how it gets its name, see?''

"Uncle Bill, I guess you know just about everything," Chuck said admiringly. "What lives in the hole in that tree?''

"Now that's one of the many things I don't know," Uncle Bill answered. "Tell you what. I'm going back to camp and get a camera. You stay here and find out the answer to your question.''

"Well, all right," Chuck agreed. "But how do I find out?''

"The same way I would," said Uncle Bill. "Watch till you see something go in or out."

"Okay," Chuck said.

He was so busy watching the hole, which was about halfway up the trunk, that he didn't even see Uncle Bill leave. After a while his neck began to ache, so he lay down on the ground and looked up. It was easier that way. But rocks kept sticking in him, and an ant crawled over his chin.

"Aw, I bet whatever's in there won't come out till tomorrow," Chuck muttered to himself. "I could climb up there and look in, I guess. That would save a lot of time."

He was pretty good at climbing trees and this one was quite easy to climb. At last he pulled himself up onto a limb that was just right. By bending a little bit he could look into the hole.

But he couldn't see anything. He tried and tried. Either his head cut off the light, or he couldn't see but an inch or two inside. He pushed his hand in and waved it around. He couldn't feel a thing. He reached further, but the sleeve of his jacket was in the way.

Chuck squatted on the branch, took off his jacket, and tied it around his neck by the sleeves. Now he could reach a long way inside. He squeezed his arm further and further down into the hole.

20

"Ow," he said aloud, because it was a tight fit.

He wriggled his fingers around in the air. This must be a pretty deep hole. What could live in it? Squirrels? A snake?

Chuck yelped and jerked his hand out of the hole. Or at least he tried to. But his arm only came out as far as his elbow. And there it stuck.

Chuck pulled and tugged. Standing on a tree limb the way he was, he was scared to pull too hard. But he was stuck and he knew it. He couldn't move his arm forward or backward. "Oh, darn!" he moaned.

He was always getting his hands and feet stuck in things. Just last week he'd had to be sawed out of a tambourine.

He guessed he was the only person in the whole wide world who'd ever got stuck in a tambourine. And he *hated* playing the tambourine; it was a baby instrument. He had wanted to play the flageolet, but Mrs. Foster, the music teacher, had said there were too many flageolets already.

When the class finished playing "The Gypsy Fire," Chuck went to put his tambourine down and he couldn't. His fingers were stuck in the little slit in the wooden frame. He asked Jimmy Johnson to help him pull it off and Jimmy tried. But he couldn't. And Mrs. Foster couldn't.

Mrs. Foster took Chuck down to the cafeteria and poured salad oil on his fingers to make them slide out. But it didn't do any good. The oil just ran down his arm and dripped on Mrs. Foster's shoes and didn't help at all.

In the end the janitor had to come and take Chuck down to the manual training room. The door to the fifth-grade room was open, and everybody stared out at Chuck and the janitor going by with the tambourine dangling between them. The janitor had to saw off the tambourine with a keyhole saw.

Mrs. Foster was mad. "This tambourine is *ruined*," she said.

And Chuck had promised himself he'd never get stuck in anything again. Now here he was fifteen feet up in the air with his arm stuck in a hole that was probably full of snakes. Oh, darn!

"Hi," said Uncle Bill. "How's the weather up there?"

Chuck looked down and grinned weakly. "Oh, fine," he said. "Uncle Bill, do you think snakes live in this hole?"

Uncle Bill looked thoughtful. "Not likely," he answered. "I think that's a flicker's hole. If the flicker doesn't use it any more, maybe a white-footed mouse lives in there, or a flying squirrel."

"Oh," said Chuck. "Do white-footed mice bite?"

"Not unless you bite them first," Uncle Bill told him. "Say, are you planning to stay up there all night?"

"I—I guess I'll have to," said Chuck mournfully. "I can't get my arm out of this hole."

"Hmmmm," said Uncle Bill.

He climbed up and stood on a branch a littler lower than the one Chuck was standing on.

"I hope this branch doesn't break," Uncle Bill said. "I'd hate to spoil all those nice bushes down below."

He reached up and pulled gently on Chuck's arm. "You really are jammed in there." He took out a pocket knife.

Chuck turned a little pale. For a minute he almost believed Uncle Bill was going to cut his arm off, for he

23

couldn't think of any other way they were going to get him out of there.

Gently Uncle Bill began to dig away at the dry wood around the edge of the hole. Chuck watched anxiously. The sun was going down. His arm hurt and he was tired of balancing on the branch. He gritted his teeth and tried not to flinch when some of the wood broke away.

"There," said Uncle Bill. "The hole's a little bigger. Now pull!"

While Uncle Bill held him, Chuck pulled hard. His arm came out slowly at first, and then in a rush. His elbow was all scraped and scratched.

He and Uncle Bill climbed down the tree and Uncle Bill looked at his arm. "We'll have to wash those scratches," he said.

"Why?" asked Chuck. "The dirt was on the outside, and the outside was the part that got scraped off."

Uncle Bill laughed. "We'll wash it, just the same, and put some antiseptic on it. Come on, we'll do that and then we'll have supper."

Chuck liked eating outside. The weenies and baked beans tasted good. And he liked the way Uncle Bill washed dishes—he just threw the paper cups and plates into the fire.

Chuck had never spent a night out in the woods before, but he kept telling himself he liked that too. The stars twinkled in a friendly way through the bare trees. The smell of dry leaves and wood smoke was sweet on the cold night air.

But it was dark as could be, not a light anywhere except the little pinpricks of stars. The crickets sounded pleasant at first. After a while it seemed to Chuck they were saying, "Watch out! Watch out! Watch out!" over and over.

Once he heard something trot by. A fox, maybe. Foxes could bite, he guessed. He scrouged down in his sleeping bag as far as he could get. Something rustled in the bushes behind him, and he craned his neck trying to get a glimpse of whatever it was.

After a while he dozed off. But he didn't sleep long. Something woke him. He couldn't see or hear Uncle Bill. He might as well be all by himself, he thought. He heard a twig snap, a rattle of leaves. He wished it wasn't quite so dark.

And then far off he heard dogs barking. At least it sounded like dogs barking, a lot of them. The sound quickly came nearer and nearer. And now it didn't sound like dogs. It sounded weird and scary and very loud. It was up in the air and all around him, a loud echoing *"Calonk, alonk, calonk!"*

Chuck made one leap out of his sleeping bag and landed on Uncle Bill.

"Uncle Bill!" he shouted. "What's that? What's that?"

"Get out of the middle of my stomach!" wheezed Uncle Bill.

Chuck rolled off Uncle Bill's sleeping bag and crouched on the bare ground. He was shivering all over. But the sound was growing faint. Whatever it was, was going away.

Uncle Bill sat up and drew a deep breath or two. "Wow!" he said. "You must have pulverized my liver."

"I'm s-sorry, Uncle Bill," Chuck stammered. "What was that noise? It scared me, it sure enough did."

"That was a flock of Canada geese going over," Uncle Bill told him. "I admit they sound a little strange at night, especially if you've never heard them before. But next time, wake me up a little more gently, will you? Somehow it upsets me to have you jumping up and down on my diaphragm."

"All right," agreed Chuck.

He got back in the sleeping bag. But he didn't go right to sleep. He lay awake for a long time, listening.

It was just barely light when he woke up. Uncle Bill already had sausages frying and biscuits baking. Chuck yawned. He guessed he hadn't had much sleep. However, he struggled up out of his sleeping bag. Breakfast smelled good and he was hungry. Besides, people always got up early on a camping trip.

Chuck took his cup of cocoa and sipped it slowly.

"I guess this is pretty far out in the woods, isn't it?" he asked at last. "I mean it's pretty wild, isn't it?"

Uncle Bill handed him a paper plate. "It'll do," he answered. "You hardly ever hear a car or a bulldozer out here, but no doubt that will come in time."

"Well, it's pretty noisy at night," said Chuck. "I mean things stirring around."

"Almost all wild creatures prefer not to be seen," said Uncle Bill. "You can count on this being a pretty lively place at night, especially in the late evenings and early mornings. That's when most of the animals are busiest

27

and most apt to be out in the open. Possums and wood rats, shrews and voles, things like that.''

Shrews and voles! A piece of Chuck's biscuit stuck in his throat, and he had to swallow hard. He might have known that a place full of crazy birds like those herons and grebes would have all sorts of other animals that nobody had ever heard of either.

''How—how big are shrews?'' he asked.

''Oh, some of them are as long as my finger,'' Uncle Bill told him. ''I'll show you one some time.'' He glanced up at Chuck and grinned. ''Most of the animals around here are very small ones. But at night when they come tramping by, they can sound like wild horses in the stillness.''

''Well, I wasn't scared,'' Chuck explained. ''I just didn't know there were so many things running around at night.'' And he and Uncle Bill laughed.

After they'd eaten, Uncle Bill got out his camera equipment and a bag like a golf bag in which he carried a telescope and some tripods and a few odds and ends.

''If those geese are anywhere around, I mean to get some pictures of them,'' he told Chuck. ''There'll be some ducks, anyway.''

They walked through the woods toward the lake. Chuck saw something moving on the water. ''Is that one?'' he whispered. ''Is that a goose, Uncle Bill?''

Uncle Bill shook his head. ''That's a coot,'' he said.

Chuck grinned. What a silly name! ''Is it crazy?'' he

28

asked, staring at the dark bird with its big white bill. He'd often heard people say someone was "crazy as a coot."

"It can sound pretty crazy when it wants to," Uncle Bill answered. "It has a big vocabulary, and it can make some funny noises when it really has something to say."

The coot wasn't saying anything now. It swam along, pumping its head back and forth and nervously watching the two people walking along the shore. Suddenly it opened its wings and got up on big greenish feet and legs. It spattered along over the surface for quite a distance before it rose into the air and flew off through the mist that lay gently over the lake.

"Gosh," said Chuck. "*That* was a crazy thing to do. I didn't know anything could walk on the water that way."

"Oh, yes," Uncle Bill told him. "A lot of water birds can't spring right up out of the water and fly. Some ducks have to run good distances before they can fly. And so do swans and geese. Though I've seen geese take off straight up in the air when they wanted to."

Chuck thought it must be fun to be able to run over the top of the water that way. He'd have to try it with his frog feet next summer.

The air was brisk and cool, but not cold. Mist curled and lifted over the lake. The tiny islands were dark spots in the fog. As they walked, Chuck could hear splashings and squawks every now and then that must have been made by some kind of bird. But he couldn't see anything.

"Look! Look, quick," whispered Uncle Bill, and Chuck had a glimpse of a black-masked face and a bushy, ringed tail.

"A raccoon!" he cried. "A real live raccoon!"

"Just like the one Davy Crockett wore," Uncle Bill

told him. "Now calm down, will you? I don't want to scare off all the ducks before the fog lifts enough for me to see them."

The sun burned out of the eastern sky. It gave the fallen leaves and the sandy shore a brassy look Chuck had never seen before. The bare tree limbs stood out blackly, and a chestnut oak that still held its leaves gleamed and glowed, a golden tree among the dark ones. The mist over the water thinned and paled.

Uncle Bill stopped close to the shore behind some bushes that made a screen. He began to set out his cameras and tripods and the telescope.

"Can I have the field glasses?" asked Chuck.

"Sure," said Uncle Bill. "You can look through the telescope when I get it set up."

Chuck hung the binoculars around his neck. He picked up something Uncle Bill had just laid down on the ground. "What's this?" he asked.

Uncle Bill chuckled. "Last time I was out here I brought a friend with me," he explained. "He said he was going to take up fishing as a hobby. He had bought himself a mighty elegant rod and a lot of flies and I don't know what all. I think a fly rod is the wrong thing to use in this lake. He'd never done any fishing, and he didn't catch a thing. Sat out there on the lake for two days and got mosquito-bitten and sunburned. He was so mad, he just shoved his fishing rod in here with all this stuff and swore he'd never go fishing again."

31

Chuck picked up the rod. "I'd like to go fishing some-time," he said.

"Well, I guess you can if you want to," said Uncle Bill absently.

Chuck put the rod down and began to examine the binoculars. He wished he had a pair of his own. What he really liked to do was to look through the wrong end. It made Uncle Bill look as if he was about a million miles away. Even Chuck's own feet were way down there. He felt like a giant.

"Now, let's see what we can see," said Uncle Bill.

The mist was almost gone. Little black blobs bobbed up and down on the water near the islands. Uncle Bill swung the telescope around and squinted into it. "Ring-neck ducks, goldeneyes, and mallards," he muttered. "But not a goose in sight. Oh, well."

"What's so wonderful about geese?" asked Chuck.

"Oh, I don't know," Uncle Bill answered. "They're such big handsome birds for one thing. And I love to hear a flock go over, with all of them speaking at once.

"Once they used to be here all year round. There are records of geese nesting here on this very river not a hundred years ago. So I feel they kind of belong around here."

"Why did they quit?" asked Chuck. "Nesting here, I mean."

"They were shot," said Uncle Bill a little grimly.

32

"Geese are odd creatures. They stick to their home grounds. Every goose summers in the neighborhood where he or she was born. When people shot the geese who nested here, no young ones were born here. So no geese came back to raise their children here. They were gone forever. Wild geese will never nest in this area again. The most we can hope for is that some will like this place well enough to spend the winter on this lake."

"Don't they stay anywhere around here?" Chuck wanted to know. He hoped they did. When Uncle Bill said the geese were gone forever, it made him feel a little sad.

"Yes, a good number of them spend the winter about a hundred miles down the river," Uncle Bill explained. "But there isn't any reason why they shouldn't stay here —at least a few of them. There's no shooting allowed, and these islands and sand bars are just what they like. And the game warden and I have planted corn out on these islands every summer for three years to attract the birds when the grain ripens in the fall." He shrugged his shoulders. "But there's no accounting for tastes. The geese just don't like it around here. They're pretty set in their ways. They don't change their habits easily."

"Where do they go in summer?" asked Chuck.

"Mostly Canada," answered Uncle Bill. "I think the ones who winter on the river come from Northern Manitoba."

"Gosh," exclaimed Chuck. "That's a long way off. Do they fly the whole way?"

"Well, flying beats walking," Uncle Bill told him. "And I haven't yet heard of one migrating by train or motor scooter."

"They could *swim* part of the way," Chuck pointed out.

Uncle Bill laughed. "So they could," he agreed. "But as far as I know, they fly all the way. Look, there are some ducks coming closer. Maybe I can get a good picture."

He peered through the telescope. The little group of ducks came nearer and nearer. Uncle Bill, moving very slowly and quietly, began to adjust his camera.

Chuck took up the field glasses, which were on a long leather string around his neck. He clapped one end to his eyes and looked hard, but he couldn't see any ducks. What he saw was an enormous black, horrible creature coming up out of the water. It spread its huge legs all over the sky. A monster!

Chuck yelled. He dropped the field glasses and sprang up out of the bushes. "Wow!" he hollered. "Uncle Bill! Uncle Bill!"

The ducks didn't wait. They rose out of the water and departed.

Uncle Bill grabbed Chuck. "What's the matter?" he cried. "What happened? Are you hurt?"

"A thing!" Chuck gasped. "A big black thing. As big

as a house. Like in a movie. It's coming up out of the water, Uncle Bill!''

Uncle Bill turned his head and stared at the lake. ''What do you mean, a thing?'' he asked. ''There's nothing in the lake. And I mean nothing. You scared off the ducks.''

Chuck had to admit there wasn't any monster in sight. ''It went back down then,'' he told Uncle Bill. ''Because I saw it, I really did. Through the field glasses.''

Uncle Bill picked up the binoculars and inspected them. ''There's your monster,'' he said.

A small gray spider crawled on the edge of one of the eyepieces.

"You must have looked through the wrong end, see? That way, if the spider was on the lens, you wouldn't be able to see anything but spider, so you thought it was a monster. Maybe you oughtn't to see so many movies."

"Oh," said Chuck feebly. "I—I guess I'm kind of dumb."

"Well, no," Uncle Bill answered and grinned at him. "Impulsive would be a better word, maybe."

Chuck brushed the spider off the glasses and put the proper end to his eyes. There wasn't anything to look at through them. The only ducks left on the water were those who'd been too far away to hear him when he hollered. He wished he hadn't been so dumb. He guessed Uncle Bill wished he hadn't brought Chuck with him.

After a while Uncle Bill picked up the rod and reel and a little plastic box of fish flies. "Here, Chuck," he said. "Why don't you take these things back to camp for me before something happens to them. Put them in the jeep. And there's a box of chocolate bars somewhere in the jeep. Help yourself and bring me one."

"All right," Chuck answered.

He got up and picked up the fishing rod and the box and set off into the woods. He was feeling rather down-hearted. Uncle Bill wasn't really worried about the fishing rod. He just wanted to get rid of Chuck.

Chuck frowned and kicked at a huckleberry bush.

He hadn't meant to scare the old ducks. And that spider had certainly looked fierce and terrible enough.

Well, if Uncle Bill didn't want him around, he wouldn't stay where he wasn't wanted. He'd go on around the edge of the lake and watch ducks by himself.

He'd fish, that's what he'd do. Uncle Bill had said he could fish if he wanted to. He'd go fishing and perhaps catch enough fish for lunch. Or anyway, catch one fish, maybe.

Chuck passed their camp and went on around the lake. He came to a place where the water ran up in a little bay. A lot of reeds and cattails grew there, and two or three buttonbushes stood in the water. It looked like a good place to fish.

He stopped and fitted the two pieces of the rod together. From the reel attached to the cork handle he unwound a piece of line and threaded it through the guides. He picked out the biggest and brightest red feathery fly and tied it to the end of the line.

Chuck knew that you were supposed to throw the fly out on the water by flicking the rod somehow. But he was scared to try it. He'd heard about a boy at school who'd hooked his own ear trying to do that. It would be just his luck to have something even worse happen. Instead, he unreeled some more of the line, took off his shoes and socks, rolled up the legs of his jeans, and waded out as far as he could go. He laid the fly carefully on the surface of the water where it floated quite nicely.

He waded back to shore and picked up the rod. That seemed a lot easier than casting, and he wondered people hadn't thought of doing it before.

Of course, the water was pretty cold. His feet were numb by the time he got out of the lake. He rubbed and rubbed and rubbed his feet and legs with his handkerchief. He got hot all over, he rubbed so hard.

Chuck put his shoes and socks back on and settled down to wait. He was tired, for he hadn't slept much the

night before, and he'd gotten up early. The sun was warm. The little wind and the lapping water were soothing. Sitting there holding the rod, he was almost asleep.

Now somebody had been watching Chuck all this time. In fact, several somebodies. And they were terribly curious. Squatting on the edge of a sand bar, they had seen him wade out into the water. They had seen him putting on his shoes and socks. And when he sat down and rested so quietly, they decided to investigate.

One, two, three, four, they slipped into the water and swam toward him. One turned back almost at once. Why waste this chance for a good nap?

The other three swam on. Their black eyes darted

here and there as they kept watch for any danger or excitement anywhere. Slowly they came over the water toward Chuck.

Chuck was very nearly asleep. He watched the big birds come closer without realizing what they were. They seemed like part of a dream. Drowsily he stared at them. Such big handsome birds with bronze-brown backs and jet-black necks and heads. When they turned their heads he could see the glistening white patches on their cheeks and throats.

Geese!

Chuck clutched the fishing rod. These must be Canada geese! Oh, he'd have something to tell Uncle Bill now. Why, they were almost close enough to touch!

He knew that, crouched in the tall grass with a bush beside him, he was almost hidden. He all but held his breath. He sat still as a mouse. One of the geese tipped up and rooted around on the bottom of the lake, looking for something to eat.

The other two looked at Chuck. They were suspicious of him. But he didn't move or make any noise. So they weren't frightened. One of them swam in a little closer.

Just then a big water beetle swam out of the reeds. The nearest goose snapped at it and missed. With a loud honk the goose dashed after the beetle. Swimming very fast, the goose followed the beetle in and out of the reeds

40

and bushes before it finally swallowed its prey. Then it straightened itself and began to swim off.

It wasn't till he felt a tug on the fishing line that Chuck realized what had happened. The fish hook had snagged on the bird's big webbed foot and instead of a fish, Chuck had caught a goose!

The goose gave an impatient honk and ruffled its feathers. It ducked its head and nibbled at the fly. And now a loop of the slackened line caught around its long neck.

Chuck stood up. "Hey!" he shouted.

With a splash and a flurry of wings the other two geese flew up and away. But the third goose could only flounder in the shallow water, honking and hissing.

Chuck pulled on the rod. The line whirred off the reel. The goose swam off toward the open water. Then it turned suddenly and flopped in among the reeds.

"Hey!" yelled Chuck again. "Leggo my line! Shoo, you old goose! Shoo!"

The goose was now thoroughly wound up in the line. It darted in and out of the reeds and bushes, winding the long nylon thread through them.

Chuck didn't know what to do. More and more of the line reeled out, in spite of his efforts to stop it. If he had a knife, he could cut the line, he thought. But he didn't have a knife. He tried holding the rod up high and

flipping the line over the tops of the cattails where it was tangled, but he couldn't do it. Instead, a brier caught on the buttons of his jacket sleeve and he thought he wasn't ever going to get loose.

42

In the meantime, the goose flopped further and further away, and Chuck had to run to catch up with it. He pulled at the line, but he knew it was useless. It was snarled around a dozen stems and branches between him and the goose.

The goose honked sadly and fearfully and seemed to sink down in the water.

"Oh, gee," Chuck groaned. "I'll *have* to wade in after him."

He didn't stop to take off his shoes and socks. He just rushed right in. The water was deeper here than it had been where he had waded out with the fly. It was well over his knees. He splashed in and out of the grasses, and the goose flopped ahead of him. Frantically, Chuck flung himself after the bird and stepped in a hole so deep the water came up to his waist. He scrambled out and got close to the goose. It stuck its head out at him and hissed dreadfully. In confusion, Chuck dropped the rod. It sank out of sight.

"Oh, help," gulped Chuck, sticking his hands down in the muddy water and feeling for the rod. He couldn't find it. He couldn't even reach the bottom. He'd have to get the goose now and untangle the line and follow it back to the rod.

He stepped toward the bird. The goose still had one wing free, and every time Chuck came close it struck at him with its wing and hissed fiercely.

Chuck was scared. This was the biggest bird he'd

ever seen. Its beak looked heavy and powerful. And those big wings could hurt, he guessed. But he was desperate. He had to get the hook out of the goose's foot, otherwise he'd never get the rod back.

Oh, he wished he'd never tried to fish. Uncle Bill hadn't really meant for him to. He should have put the rod in the jeep the way he'd been told.

He *had* to catch that goose. He took a step toward it, and the goose struck at him again and again with its wing.

Chuck drew a deep breath, grabbed, and held on tight. All he got was feathers. A bunch of big feathers came loose in his hands. The goose squawked and honked and splashed.

"Oh, gosh," yelled Chuck. "Wait a minute! Wait a minute!" He grabbed again and got some more feathers.

"What in the blue blazes is going on here?" somebody asked.

Chuck jumped. He had a feeling whoever owned that deep voice didn't think he ought to be here fishing for geese. He was almost too mad and tired and scared to care. He turned around. A man was standing there, a big man with a tanned and weather-beaten face, and a wide-brimmed hat and a badge.

The game warden!

Chuck knew that's who it was. He'd be in sure-enough trouble now. He wished Uncle Bill was here.

"I guess I'll have to arrest you for goose-hunting out of season," the game warden said.

44

He stepped into the shallow water and picked up the goose. Holding the bird expertly under one arm, he untangled the line, located the rod and reel, and waded back to shore.

"I wasn't hunting," burst out Chuck. "I was *fishing*. And the old goose just caught himself."

"Hmmmm," said the game warden. "You got a license to fish?"

Chuck flushed. "I didn't know you needed one," he said. Harder than ever he wished Uncle Bill was here.

The game warden worked the fishhook out of the goose's foot and unwound the line from around the big legs and body.

"Fishing without a license is a pretty serious charge," he said slowly.

"I was only pre—pretending to fish," Chuck stammered. "Honest, I didn't mean to catch anything, not even a goose."

"Chuck!" called Uncle Bill. "Are you all right? Where are you?"

"We're over here, Bill," yelled the game warden. "We're okay."

Chuck felt better. That didn't sound as if the game warden meant to do anything too bad to him. And he was sure glad to see Uncle Bill.

Uncle Bill came up to them. "Did you fall in, Chuck?" he asked. "You look like it."

46

Chuck realized for the first time that he was wet from head to toe. And cold, now that he stopped to think of it. He shivered.

"This a friend of yours?" asked the game warden, nodding at Chuck.

"He's my nephew," explained Uncle Bill. "Chuck, this is Mr. Jim Andrews, the game warden. Say, where'd you get the goose? Did Chuck swim after him?"

"Nope," Mr. Andrews answered, and he grinned. "Caught him with a fly rod." And he told Uncle Bill what had happened.

"Well, I'll be switched," said Uncle Bill.

The goose honked mournfully and looked at them as if to ask how in the world he ever got in this situation.

"I'm going to take the goose back to my place," said the game warden. "It doesn't look hurt, but I want to be sure. And I want to weigh it and band it. And you better take that nephew back to your place and get him some dry clothes."

"You're right, Jim," agreed Uncle Bill.

"Then you two come over and see me," said Mr. Andrews. "I'll let Chuck give me a few pointers on catching geese."

Uncle Bill laughed and led his dripping nephew through the woods back to camp. When Chuck was dry and warm and drinking cocoa by the fire, he looked up at Uncle Bill and said sadly, "I'm sorry. I shouldn't have

used the rod. But I didn't mean to catch the goose. I was just sort of playing."

"Well, next time you might ask," Uncle Bill said. "It wasn't my rod, you know. I did say you could fish, but I didn't mean now, and I didn't mean by yourself. However, I don't think the rod's hurt or the goose either."

"I guess you won't ever take me camping again," Chuck went on gloomily. "I've been so much trouble this time."

"Oh, not all that much trouble," Uncle Bill said. "And

as for catching the goose . . . well, that was partly the goose's fault, I suppose. In fact, I think you and that goose have something in common. I suspect that goose gets into trouble once in a while too.''

"How could a goose get into trouble?" asked Chuck.

"Well, I'll tell you about it," said Uncle Bill thoughtfully. "Get comfortable and I'll tell you about this goose from the very beginning, way up in Manitoba. And a goose, of course, begins with an egg. And an egg begins with a mother goose and a father gander and a nest . . .''

Chen

THE goose built her nest in a beaver meadow, on top of an old beaver house. It was a good nest, hollowed out of leaves and twigs and lined with soft goose down. When the nest was done, she laid five good-sized dull white eggs in it.

After that she sat on the eggs. She sat on them for twenty-eight days. It was a long time, but the weather was pleasant and she had nothing else in particular to do.

The gander stayed close by in case of danger.

Once in a while an old beaver came to see her. The beaver house had been his a long time ago, and he liked to come back and look at it every now and then. The goose didn't mind the beaver swimming by. But if he tried to climb up on the pile of sticks and mud, she laid her neck out flat and opened her beak wide and hissed at him. He always went away then.

After all those days the first egg hatched. The goose stood up and looked at the gosling. He was very handsome, just what she'd expected. She admired him for several minutes. Then she pushed the shell of the egg out of the nest and sat down again.

50

A crow who was flying by swooped down and grabbed
up the egg shell. Quick as lightning, the goose shot her
neck out at him and hissed ferociously. She ruffled her
feathers and hunched her wings forward and made her-
self look as big as a bear.

The crow took a backward step in the air and almost
turned over. The eggshell fell into the water and sank,
and the crow flew off and lit in a bush.

"*Caw! Haw! Haw!*" he called. He had known all

along it was just an empty eggshell. There was no need for anybody to raise such a fuss.

By nighttime all the eggs had hatched. The last-born gosling crouched, wet and wobbly, in the bottom of the nest. This was Chen. Chen was not his name, but it will do, for he had no name of his own.

Chen and his brother and his three sisters drowsed in the dark warmth of the nest all that night and the next day and the next night.

The second morning the sun shone down hot and bright. The old beaver climbed out on the bank to sit in the sun and eat a few twigs. The sky was blue and cloudless. The beaver squatted down with half-closed eyes. He could smell the flat smell of water and mud, the sweet smell of new grass and green things, and a faint sharp scent of balsam from some far-off place.

The goose stood up and inspected her new family. The beaver dropped his twig and watched. That goose and her nest irritated him. He would be glad when they were gone.

The goose whispered to her children. She was going to eat breakfast, and she wanted them to be good while she was away. She wanted them to be quiet and safe.

The goslings settled down in the bottom of the nest. The goose honked twice, spread her wings, and flew. Her wings made a loud rushing noise.

The beaver slid into the water and swam toward the

nest. Something had happened, he knew. He meant to find out what it was. He slowly came closer and peered up at the nest.

The goslings were good children. They were quiet as their mother had meant them to be. Only Chen stretched his neck to stare around at the sun on the water, the scrubby willows, and the beaver swimming by.

Two of his sisters, feeling chilly, shoved hard, one on each side of Chen. Chen was just leaning out of the nest to get a better look at the beaver. With a single frightened squeak he toppled over the edge of the nest, down the sloping roof of the beaver house, and into the water.

Chen was surprised to find himself in the water, but he wasn't scared. His feet knew just what to do. They paddled round and round and he was swimming.

But something did scare him a little. He was all by himself in the lake. He looked around, peeping sadly. Somebody should have been there with him. Somebody big and dark.

There! Perhaps that was what he was hunting for. It was big and it was dark and it was swimming in the water with him. Chen paddled after the beaver.

The beaver turned and swam away. He didn't want to have anything to do with goslings. He didn't like geese.

Chen peeped louder. He swam closer to the beaver.

The beaver looked over his shoulder and muttered through his big teeth. Why didn't this little screaming creature go away?

Chen paddled faster. Wasn't he supposed to keep up with this thing, even if it had such a curious tail and such a strange beak? He opened his own beak and cried louder than ever. The beaver whirled in the water and almost upset Chen with his tail.

Chen might have gone on and tried to be a little beaver except that his mother had heard him peeping so forlornly. She was coming back to see what was wrong. She landed in the water with a great hissing and honking and flapping of wings. She had been suspicious of this beaver all along. And now he was trying to go off with one of her goslings!

The beaver dived under the water. Chen rocked in the ripples that the goose's angry approach had made and murmured happily. This was a better mother than that

other one with the funny tail. The goose touched him
with her bill and whispered to him.

The goose had not meant to take her family into the
water so early in the day. But now there was no help for
it. She did not think about putting Chen back in the nest.
Once one gosling got out, all of them must get out. She
called softly, and the other goslings tumbled into the
water.

The gander came swimming toward them. He spread
his great wings and honked a happy welcome to his
children.

The beaver watched them line up, first the goose,
then the goslings, last the gander, keeping a careful watch
for danger. When they had sailed away, he climbed up
on the beaver house and scattered the nest in all direc-
tions. He looked as if he were telling himself that no
goose had better try to build a nest here again. He'd
pull her tail feathers out.

All that sunny day the goslings swam about on the
lake learning to eat. The goose and the gander helped

them to find flies and gnats. There were tiny seeds and tender grass to eat too. Chen was very lucky and accidentally swallowed a tadpole.

By afternoon he was tired. The goose called her children up on the shore and settled them under her big wings for the night.

The next day the goose decided to move her family. She knew of a neighborhood where there was better food for young goslings and more reeds to hide in and deeper water to dive in. This was a fine place for nesting, but it wasn't the place to raise a family.

It was a long walk to their new home, almost two miles. There were deep holes to fall into and sticks to jump over and bushes to walk around. The sun was hot and the way was rough. Goslings don't like to walk. Their legs are better for swimming than for walking long distances. Chen's short legs grew very tired and he squatted down to rest. His brothers and sisters rested, too, while his father and mother kept watch for danger.

And there was danger. Not the beavers, no. Nobody feared the beavers. But there were gulls and crows. And a skunk who lived in a burrow under the willow bushes, and a duck hawk with streaked breast. Any one of these might have killed the goslings and eaten them.

However, the goose and the gander knew how to watch out for these enemies, how to drive them off if they came too near. There was only one animal of which

the geese were really afraid. It went on two legs and carried a gun.

Still, men seldom came here. There was not much need to worry about them.

Chen didn't worry about being eaten. He worried about eating. He was hungry. A gnat came flying by, and Chen reached up to grab it, but one of his sisters got there first. She swallowed it with a neat snap of her bill.

Chen had been sure he was going to get that gnat. He had been so ready to swallow that he had to go on and swallow anyway. Nothing at all went down, and it wasn't nearly so satisfactory as the gnat would have been.

There was a little new blade of grass growing right beside him. He could eat that. But just as he reached out for it, the goose gave the signal that it was time to start walking again. So Chen walked.

It took nearly the whole day to reach the new lake. When they got close, the goose urged the goslings along faster than ever. Soon they would be safe in the water. Chen was so tired it was almost more than he could do to pick up his big wide-webbed feet. He kept stumbling and falling down.

Once he fell down and when he got up he couldn't walk. Instead he fell down again. Something had hold of his foot.

A piece of vine had twisted around his leg and held him fast. He pulled away from it, and it jerked him back and made him sit down hard. His brothers and sisters sat down too and went quietly to sleep.

Chen peeped sadly. The gander walked up and stared at his family. The goose whispered to Chen, urging him to come along quickly.

Chen would have been glad to come along, only he couldn't. He could tell that his mother was impatient and a little frightened, and that scared him more than ever. In a panic he pulled and tugged at the vine.

The goose peered down at Chen. She did not like having one of her children behave this way. She knew something was wrong, but she wasn't quite sure what. She began to walk anxiously around Chen, looking him over. If she could not make him get up by standing on one side of him, perhaps she could by standing on the other. She came so close she almost stepped on him and scared him worse than ever.

No matter how she tried, the goose couldn't make Chen walk. She was getting more and more excited. She tramped back and forth—and stepped on the tautened vine. With a juicy "pop!" the vine snapped. Chen felt the hold on his leg slacken. He was free!

He staggered to his feet. His mother was a little surprised. What could have cured him so suddenly? She didn't stop to ponder it, however. She just hurried him toward the lake.

The gander walked on with the other goslings. They

had rested a little and they walked fast. The water was quite near. But Chen and the goose trailed far behind. Chen was just about worn out and he still had a long piece of the vine tangled around his leg. He kept stepping on it and tripping himself up.

At last the goose and the gosling reached the shore. The gander and Chen's brother and sisters were already sailing on the lake. The water was cool. It felt wonderful to Chen to be swimming and floating, not walking on his weary stumbling feet. The air was full of gnats and flies and other good things to eat. Chen ducked his head happily in the ripples. Already he had almost forgotten the long hike and his accident.

The gander too was glad to see his family safe upon the lake. He too was tired and hungry. Especially hungry, for he had been so busy he'd scarcely had time to eat all day. A fresh and tender-looking tendril of vine floated on the water. That might make part of his supper. The gander picked it up and began to chew a leaf.

The vine was heavy. More than that, it shrieked. Chen, hoisted in the air by the vine tangled around his leg, kicked and screamed. Just as he had thought he was safe this dreadful thing had happened to him. He hung upside down and did the only thing he could do, which was to yell.

Chen's father was frightened. He didn't like having a piece of green vine shrieking under his chin. He shook

his head in alarm. Chen, swinging on the end of the vine, saw the world rock back and forth. He yelled louder than ever.

The goose honked. The gander shook his head faster

and faster. Chen peeped wildly and the other goslings swam hither and thither in panic. Suddenly Chen's foot slipped from the vine. He fell into the water with a little splash. As he bobbed up, he said nothing at all. He was too tired and scared and sore even to squeak.

The gander slowly swallowed the rest of the vine. It tasted fine for a vine that had behaved so strangely.

Chen was glad to go to bed. Under his mother's warm down he forgot the ache in his leg and how scared and tired he had been. He closed his eyes and slept.

Where Chen lived, the summer days were long and the nights were short. A gosling spent a lot of his time growing. He ate and slept and swam. Once in a while Chen and his brother and sisters played a game of tag in the water. But never a very long game. And they hardly ever squabbled. It is a funny thing how much time you have when you don't spend any of it fighting with your brothers and sisters.

So Chen had plenty of time for learning. He learned not to go too near the long-legged great blue heron, who might have mistaken him for a frog and stabbed him with its huge bill. He learned to dive when his mother gave the whistling call that meant danger. And to swim in among the reeds and stay hidden till she gave the signal that it was safe to come out.

Chen learned that when the loons laughed and

laughed and the wind blew a certain way and the air
had a certain feel, a storm was on the way. And he learned
to seek shelter from the pelting rain and the chilly wind
that bent the bushes and laid the grass flat and turned the
ripples on the lake into waves.

Before he was three weeks old, Chen learned a private lesson of his own. He was sleeping in the sun one day when two gulls flew over. One was carrying a small fish in its beak, and the other tried to snatch this tasty morsel away. For a moment the two birds hung in the air, struggling fiercely. The little fish slipped from its pos-sessor's grasp and flipped down through the air. It landed with a thud on Chen's back.

Chen, startled out of a dream of duckweed, could only wheeze and gasp. The first gull swooped down and grabbed up its fish and flew off.

The second gull stayed long enough to tell Chen what a stupid goose he was to get in the way of falling fish. And then it flew away too. Chen stood up and shook himself all over. He complained for a while, and then he went to sleep again.

But his back was sore for several days. And after that he always looked to make sure it wasn't raining fish before he took a nap.

There were some other goose families on the lake. Once in a while Chen glimpsed them or heard them. But his family never visited with another family. In fact, if two goose families came near each other, there was a great deal of honking and hissing and flapping of wings until all the young ones scattered and disappeared and the two families were once more separated by a wide stretch of water.

64

However, one day not long after the day it rained fish, Chen was surprised to wake up and find two strange geese eating grass right beside him. Neither his father nor his mother seemed disturbed by these newcomers.

But Chen was disturbed. And so was his brother. They were excited and a little frightened. And just as their parents did when something upset them, Chen and his brother spread their wings and laid their necks out flat and hissed squeakily at the strangers. The two new geese stepped a little distance away from the goslings and went on eating quietly.

The two goslings were pleased with themselves. They raised their necks and wings and then bowed to each other proudly. They were growing up. They knew how to treat intruders. They felt they had done just the right thing.

The two new geese didn't go away, however, which might have hurt Chen's feelings if he'd stopped to think about it. In fact, the next day there were three more strange geese eating grass. And though Chen didn't know it, they were really part of the family. They were his older brothers and sisters, born the year before and the year before that, not yet old enough to have mates and families of their own.

There was also an elderly gander, who was Chen's uncle. He was a bachelor who had never been able to find a mate to suit him. Chen did not care too much for this uncle. Whenever Chen found a particularly fresh and tender patch of grass, or a bush that was heavily loaded with berries, or some especially delicious roots, the uncle would always appear and shove Chen aside and help himself to the feast. It was very annoying.

The older geese kept dropping their feathers all over the place. The feathers littered the shores and floated on the lake. Sometimes Chen picked up one in his bill and turned it over and over thoughtfully. Maybe he was puzzled about why anybody would want to throw away such perfectly good, great big beautiful feathers. His own feathers were just beginning to come in, and he took very good care of them.

The older brothers and sisters and the uncle spent a

lot of their time hiding in the reeds and lying quietly in the grass. Now that they had molted their feathers, they couldn't fly. It was a dangerous time, for a goose must often depend on his wings to carry him away from danger. So they made themselves as inconspicuous as possible.

Besides, growing new feathers is hard work. It made the geese feel quiet and lazy.

Soon Chen's mother and father began to shed their feathers, too. The big wing feathers came out almost all at once. And then they too were flightless.

Now everybody spent the long summer days drifting quietly among the grasses and reeds. Each goose rested and grew new plumage. For Chen and the other young ones were growing up. As the summer drew to an end,

it was hard to tell the young geese from the old ones. At least from a distance.

Close up, one could see that Chen's colors were not so deep nor so bright as those of his parents and his older brothers and sisters. His markings were not so clear and clean-cut. But he was no longer a gosling. He was a goose, with a black head and long black neck and a white cheek patch. He could even honk in a squeaky way.

He couldn't fly yet, however. At this season, none of the geese could fly. Chen didn't mind. He didn't know that not being able to fly was dangerous. He didn't even know he was ever going to be able to fly. Flying was something mothers and fathers did.

He enjoyed the long hot days. And he liked sleeping among the rushes, with the wind rattling them gently overhead. Sometimes he met a frog among the reeds. A frog was a curious creature. If you came up close, it said "Quork!" and leaped in a long curve into the water.

There were minnows in the lake. If Chen could catch one of these little fish, he ate it. He didn't often try. He preferred to eat the water plants and snails and roots that couldn't swim away. And they tasted very good. And so did the big water bugs that whirled in and out of the reeds. Chen especially liked water bugs.

The days went by and the feathers grew. On warm windy days the grown-up geese came out of the reeds and stood around flapping their great wings and honking a

little, as though they were going to take off any minute. But their wings weren't quite strong enough.

And then one sunny morning toward the end of August, almost all the old geese got up and flapped and flapped—and flew. With a great rush of wings there were geese flying everywhere, practicing with their new feathers.

Chen was excited. He stood on tiptoe and flapped his wings too. And Chen flew! He took a few running steps and beat his wings, and all of a sudden he was flying! He wiggled and wobbled through the air—and flew straight into his uncle!

Uncle and nephew tumbled to the ground in a heap. The uncle stood up and hissed loudly and struck Chen again and again with his wings. Poor Chen crouched on the ground and trembled.

The uncle waddled off and stood by himself a minute. Grumbling softly, he ruffled his feathers and then settled them neatly around his body. He preened his new flight feathers and honked in a loud, severe voice. And then he flew out across the lake.

But Chen didn't fly. He walked away and sat under a bush. Even when he saw his brother and sisters flying over the water, he only stared and shook his head a little. He didn't try to fly again for a whole day.

After that he flew a lot, back and forth across the lake, along the little river, out over the grassy plain. He was strengthening his wings and learning all that a goose has to know about flying.

He was learning, too, to look out for himself. When he was on one side of the lake and his mother was on the other, he could hardly expect her to warn him of danger. He began to spend more time watching with his round black eyes and to be more suspicious of strange sights and sounds.

One day as he was walking through the tall grass he
came face to face with a fox. The fox smiled pleasantly,
and his fluffy tail drooped softly behind him.

But Chen wasn't fooled. This was danger and he
knew it. He froze in his tracks and tried to make himself
look like a piece of driftwood, because this is what young
geese do when they meet danger.

The fox wasn't fooled either. He recognized a good
dinner when he saw it. He stretched out his neck till his
nose almost touched Chen. With a wild squawk Chen

remembered his wings. He ran right over the fox and flew
off, calling triumphantly. The fox smiled a little more and
trotted off into the grass.

Now the days were growing shorter and the nights
were cold. In the bright mornings the wind swept over
the lake, icy and sharp. It made Chen restless and excited.
He raised himself in the water, flapping his wings and
honking. Across the lake another goose answered. And
then another and another.

72

Sometimes flocks of ducks went over, and once in a while a flock would land on the lake. The ducks would stay close together, quacking nervously to each other about something. And then Chen would ruffle his feathers, as though an uneasy tingle had gone over him. He and the other geese would fidget about over the lake, looking for something, but not sure what it was.

One day a big V of geese went over, honking sweetly among themselves. Chen honked back and suddenly he sprang into the air. He circled the lake in the cold wind and landed once more in the water.

Now all the geese knew. It was time to go.

The next day Chen's whole family left the lake. They flew only a short way, to a larger river. Several hundred geese were already gathered there.

They stayed on the river a few days while more and more geese streamed out of the sky. Ducks flew over, one flock after another. All night and all day the air was full of squeaks, hisses, quacks, murmurs, honks, and the whistle of wings.

Then one cold, still morning the river was trimmed and edged in ice. Chen's mother and father, his brothers and sisters, his uncle, and some cousins stood on a sand bar, holding their heads high and looking, looking, looking off into the distance.

Suddenly the uncle shook his head twice. He raised his wings in a sort of shrug, spread them wide, took a few quick steps, and was flying. One by one the other geese flew behind him in a long sloping line. Chen came last of all. But his mother dropped behind him and urged him up to the others.

They flew fast and they flew far. By nightfall they were a long way from the river where Chen had seen ice for the first time.

Chen had no idea where he was going. But the older geese knew. They had made this journey often before. One or the other of the older geese always took the hard position at the head of the flock, leading the way over the wooded valleys and hills. Sometimes they flew in a long line and sometimes in a V. Sometimes they were silent and sometimes they called out to each other, in warning or encouragement.

Chen and the other young geese needed encouragement. This was their first long flight and they were tired by the end of the day.

They landed on a lake. There was plenty to eat around the edges of the lake, grass and seeds and roots. They stayed there almost a week before they set out again.

This time they flew at night. Against the starry sky the dark V of the flock sailed through the night like an arrow. Chen, looking down, could see the shadowy forests, the dully gleaming rivers. They flew over a little town with lights shining in the houses. Chen stared. He'd never seen such a thing before.

The river where they landed was broad and deep, but there was very little to eat there. They rested a day and a night and then flew on.

It took over a month to make the trip. Once in a while they would travel a long way and then spend several days feeding and resting. Then for a while they flew short distances every day.

Once they flew straight into a great fog. The white cloud billowed over them before there was time to turn aside or fly above it. In seconds they were lost in the mist.

The geese called out to each other anxiously. The leader could no longer spy out the landmarks which showed the way. They lost their sense of direction and flew in aimless circles. The flock bunched closer together, for they preferred to be lost all together, not lost one by one.

Chen was flying last in the line. He was tired and had straggled a little behind the others. When the rest of the geese honked, he answered and tried to keep up with them.

But all this thick white swirling stuff bewildered him. He kept twisting and turning, hoping to find a hole in it. His family had disappeared, and now even the sounds of their voices were fading. He honked louder than ever and faint answers seemed to come now from this side, now from that.

The truth of the matter was that while the rest of

the flock had mounted higher, Chen had drifted lower and lower. Frightened and confused, Chen flew swiftly on.

He wasn't afraid of flying into a cliff or a building. He didn't know such things could happen, but he was afraid of the fog and afraid of being separated from the flock.

Something big and dark loomed up just beneath him in the fog. And then another and another. A sense of ground and grass came up to Chen. Something told him to land here. He braked with his wings and skidded into the wet grass. The big dark things blew out their breath at him and moved uneasily around.

They were cows, and they made Chen as uncomfortable as he made them. He scuttled in and out among their feet, honking dismally and holding his wings half-open.

The cows milled about in the mist. Chen's honks scared them a little, but they were curious about him. They crowded close. Their legs were like a forest to Chen.

He wanted to fly, but he was afraid of the fog. He spread his wings, and the cows brushed against him and upset him. One of them put a big hoof almost on him.

Chen flopped away like a huge feather duster. He slid down a muddy bank into the watering pond. He paddled out to the middle of the pond and floated there, sulky and frightened. He felt he was fairly safe on the water. After a long time, he tucked his head under his wing and slept.

In the morning the fog was gone. But Chen was still lost. There wasn't a goose in sight. The cows, knee-deep in the pond, looked at him curiously. Chen gave them an angry stare and flew off. He went south because south was the way he should go. But that was all he knew.

At last he found a river. He flew along it as it wound in and out among the fields and farmlands. And finally he saw geese. Where a small river flowed into the one Chen was following, there was a small sandy beach. On the beach and in the river were hundreds of ducks and geese. With a happy "Calonk!" Chen landed among them.

But his family wasn't there. Chen felt very forlorn.

No one was mean to him, none of these new geese tried to drive him away. But they were strangers. Nobody welcomed him. He swam up to one family, and they all suddenly turned their backs on him and swam quietly out into the middle of the river.

Chen gazed after them. A water bug floated by and he ate it. Then all at once he flew again. He didn't like being with these geese who were not his relatives.

He flew up the river, over fields from which the corn had already been harvested. Here and there groups of geese were feeding on the waste grain left behind among the dried stalks. And suddenly Chen saw a flock which he was certain was his family.

He circled, calling to them. And sure enough his mother and father looked up and honked back. Hastily Chen banked and turned and landed.

Unfortunately he landed in the field next to the one where his family was feeding. A wire fence separated the two fields. Chen could see the fence. But it hardly seemed to be there at all. He didn't suspect that all those little thin strings of something could hold him back.

However, they did. He pushed against the wire and pushed against it. Nothing happened. He honked and flapped his wings and pushed some more, but the fence was firm. He couldn't get through it.

It was provoking. He'd been separated from his family for a long time and he had missed them very much. Now here they were, so close, and yet he could not get to them.

And besides that, he was very hungry. One water bug hardly fills up a growing goose. And beyond the fence there was plenty to eat. If only this thing didn't keep holding him and shoving him away.

He ran frantically up and down the wires, sticking his head through, first here and then there. He pushed hard against the fence, clawing at it with his big feet and

flapping his wings. He squeezed and squeezed, but at last he had to give up. Panting and wheezing, he stood with his long head and neck on one side of the wires, and his wings and feet and body on the other.

His mother walked over to him and sat down to keep him company. She looked at him rather sadly and shook her head. Chen honked gloomily. He could see all that good corn lying on the ground. Close to the fence, almost close enough for him to reach it, there was a whole heap of yellow grain.

Just then Chen's uncle walked up and began to eat this particular pile of corn. He would nibble a few grains and then lift his black head and look around, keeping watch for hunters or farmers or anybody else who might want to harm a goose.

The sight infuriated Chen. He drew his head back from between the wires and squawked indignantly. He waved his wings and jumped into the air. When he came down, he was on the other side of the fence.

For a minute he was so surprised to find the wires gone he couldn't move. He just stood still, holding his wings a little away from his body and muttering softly to himself.

The world was full of surprises. But next time he found a fence between him and something he wanted, he would know to jump over it.

He began to pick up grains of corn among the fallen

stalks. His mother joined him and they ate happily together.

That night there was a heavy frost. Ice formed in ponds and puddles close to the river. But no one cared. They were almost at the end of their journey.

They set out through the cold, still air, clamoring to each other in their wild voices. Higher and higher they climbed, turning and wheeling in the air currents. Below them the fields and the river turned and wheeled too, growing smaller and smaller as the flock rose through the clear sky.

Chen's father led the way. There was a swampy lake half a day's flight from here where they would spend the night.

But something had happened during the summer. The lake was gone. Where sycamore and hackberry trees had grown along the banks, there were only big stumps. And where the lake had been, there was only raw ugly dirt and great red-and-yellow machines roaring and pushing the earth about.

The geese circled the place in fear and puzzlement. Finally the flock flew on. Twice they turned back, looking at the place where they had meant to land, searching for the familiar lake. But it was gone. At last the geese climbed higher in the sky and went on. They were anxious to get to their winter home after this disappointment.

This country was much more settled than the country Chen was used to. There were far more houses and farms, roads, cities, automobiles, and people. All the geese were uneasy. They flew the rest of the day and half the night. They were only a little distance from their wintering grounds now. But they had made a long flight, and the young ones were very tired. They had to rest.

Here was a place where the river was dammed and widened into a lake. Here was shelter on islands and sand bars, and probably food. The geese circled, calling out to each other uncertainly. Was this a good place? Was it safe?

At last they set their wings and glided to the water. This was a good, safe place. They could stay here.

As soon as the sun rose, the geese fed on the corn on the islands. As the day went on they gathered on the sand bars beyond the islands, toward the open water, and rested.

Chen and his brother and two of his sisters explored a little. They swam from one island to another and saw some ducks and a few crows and killdeers.

At last they settled down on a little beach and stared toward the shore. Something was going on over there. Some creature kept fidgeting along the bank. It waded out into the water and splashed back. It waved things about. And finally it settled down quietly by a bush.

Chen couldn't stand it. He had to get a closer look at

that creature. He walked into the water and began to swim. His brother and sisters followed. But one of the sisters turned back. She was too sleepy to care.

As they silently sailed closer, Chen stared and stared. Whatever the thing was, it was very still and looked harmless. What a curious little heap of a thing it was, with a long stick sticking out of it!

Chen came closer and closer. The thing was so still he almost lost interest in it. When a water bug swam by, he dived after it. When he had captured the bug and turned back toward the others, something tugged at his foot. He ducked his head and nibbled at it, and when he straightened up, something tightened around his neck. . . .

Chuck and Chen

"AND you know the rest," Uncle Bill finished as he got up to see if Chuck's jacket was dry. "Want some more cookies?"

"No, thanks," said Chuck. He was thoughtful. "Do you really think that goose had so many things happen to him?"

Uncle Bill laughed. "Now, how should I know?" he asked. "I never met that goose before this morning. But a goose is like a boy, I guess. None of them grow up without getting into some trouble."

"But do you think any goose could get into as much trouble as I do?" Chuck wanted to know.

Uncle Bill turned the jacket, stirred up the fire, and sat down again.

"Well, every one of those things I told you about has happened to geese or ducks I know of. But in some ways a goose is different from a boy. A boy can get into all kinds of messes with fishing rods and tambourines and still not be in any great danger. If a goose does the wrong thing, it's likely to be the end of the goose. So I suppose a goose with your impulsive ways would be a dead goose before he was six weeks old, unless he was exceptionally lucky."

Chuck frowned. "I might have known you were just making all that up to make me feel better," he complained. "Nobody has bad luck the way I do."

"Do you have such bad luck?" Uncle Bill asked.

"It seems that way to me," Chuck answered glumly. "I don't mean to do the wrong thing, but somehow it just always happens. I turn over lots of ink and milk and things. And one time I was at Johnny Parker's and when I washed my hands, the faucet in the basin just broke off. And the water kept coming out and coming out and Johnny's mother couldn't find the place to cut the water off in the basement and Johnny's father had to come home from work and turn it off. And it wasn't my fault. I just barely touched the old faucet."

Chuck wadded up his paper cup and napkin and threw them into the fire. Then he went on.

"And when Miss Latimore asked me to put the basketball in the storeroom at school, the wind blew the door shut. It never had happened before. And there isn't any knob on the inside. It was about an hour before somebody remembered where I was and got me out of there. And there isn't any light in there either, or any place to sit down except on the floor."

"You do have a tale of woe," Uncle Bill told him cheerfully. "But you'll grow out of it, I expect. People generally do. Your jacket's dry. Get your shoes on, and

85

we'll go see this unlucky goose. Sure you don't want any
more cookies?''

Chuck shook his head. Just thinking about how unlucky he was, sort of took away his appetite. It wasn't
till he had his shoes and jacket on that he decided he
could eat some more. Fishing for geese is hungry work.
He decided he'd better take the box of cookies with him.

He and Uncle Bill climbed into the jeep. "Anyway,"
said Chuck, "it would be nice if I could do the right
thing once in a while. Even if I did it by accident, it
would be nice."

"Just keep plugging," Uncle Bill advised him. "The time is bound to come."

Privately, Chuck thought it couldn't happen soon enough to suit him.

They drove out of the woods and bounced down the road. Chuck was a little scared about seeing the game warden. He couldn't help remembering what Mr. Andrews had said about fishing without a license being a serious offense. He didn't suppose he'd have to go to jail. But he guessed he'd have to pay a fine. And just when he'd got almost enough money saved to buy a rocket, the kind you shot off with water and vinegar and baking powder or something like that.

Mr. Andrews lived in a rackety little house close to the water. Chuck thought it was pretty keen. There was hardly any furniture in it. Though Mr. Andrews' big desk and his bookcase seemed to be orderly and neat, everything else was the way Chuck liked it, piled up all over.

There were birds' nests and birds' eggs on everything, and a cage with two bedraggled ducks in it in one corner. There was an outboard motor on the floor and a lot of magazines stacked around. And a fox's skin and a bushel of corn and some guns and a can of kerosene with a potato stuck on the spout.

Chuck didn't know a game warden would have all these interesting things around him. He had thought

game wardens didn't do anything but walk around arresting people who were shooting ducks at the wrong time of year.

And deer too. In movie cartoons and in funny papers, people were always getting in trouble with the game warden about shooting deer and moose. Chuck didn't think there were any moose around here. But maybe there were deer. He'd have to ask Uncle Bill if there were any deer in these woods.

88

And if there were, *he* wasn't going to get mixed up with them. Anybody who could get into such a mess with a goose . . . no telling what would happen to him if he ever ran into a deer.

Uncle Bill talked for a few minutes to Mr. Andrews. Then he waved a hand at Chuck, who was looking for a place to sit down that wasn't covered with birds' nests or boxes of shotgun shells. He finally had to sit down on the edge of a chair which already had on it a big bird's nest containing two eggs.

"I brought the culprit," said Uncle Bill. "He's all dry now, and you can pronounce sentence."

Chuck's heart beat faster. He wanted to believe Uncle Bill was kidding. But was he?

The game warden looked at Chuck. "Maybe I'll make him sit on that nest of hawk eggs and hatch them," he said. So Chuck knew it was all right. "It looks as if he's aiming to do it anyway."

He picked up a notebook and turned the pages. "I hate to tell the Wildlife Service I've banded a goose somebody caught on a fly rod," he complained. "But I guess I'll have to."

He read out, "One Ungava Canada Goose, male, age approximately six months, weight six and one-half pounds, condition good, no evidence of injury or disease . . ." He broke off and gave Chuck a stern look. "I think the least you could do now is to go out and tell the critter you're sorry. Think how humiliated he must be, being caught like a trout."

"Sh-sure," stammered Chuck. Where is he?"

Mr. Andrews laughed. "He's penned outside," he said. He picked up a little aluminum band and a pair of pliers. "We'll go put this band on him, and then I want to show you something."

Chuck examined the band. "What's it for?" he asked.

Mr. Andrews showed him the numbers on it and the words, "Notify Fish and Wildlife Service, Washington, D.C."

"I've made a record of his number and where he was captured and so forth," Mr. Andrews explained. "I'll send it off to Washington and they'll file the information away. Now if somebody shoots this goose or finds him dead somewhere and then sends that little band or the number from it to the Wildlife Service, we'll know a little something more about where geese travel and how they live."

Chuck was indignant. "Nobody had better shoot that goose," he cried.

"Well, somebody might catch him with a fishing rod," the game warden said.

"Oh, Uncle Bill, couldn't we keep him?" begged Chuck. "I don't want anybody to shoot him."

Uncle Bill shook his head. "We couldn't keep him.

He'd rather be shot than penned up, I think," he told Chuck. "But if we could persuade him to stay around here, he needn't be shot—at least not this winter. There's no shooting allowed around the lake, you know."

Oh, gosh, thought Chuck as they went outside. Maybe he would have stayed if I hadn't caught him. I guess now he'll leave because I've scared him and he thinks we're all trying to be mean to him.

The goose—whom Chuck now thought of as Chen— did look scared and miserable, as though he thought everybody was trying to be mean to him. He crouched in one corner of the pen and when Chuck and the two men came close, he tried to jump out. There was wire netting over the top of the cage so, of course, he couldn't.

It *must* be Chen, thought Chuck. He knows about trying to fly over a fence.

But Chen didn't seem to recognize Chuck. He merely honked sadly and flapped his wings as Mr. Andrews reached in the pen and grabbed him. The game warden turned the goose upside down and tucked Chen under his arm so that the goose's long black neck snaked out behind him. Chen's wings were safely closed, and his legs stuck up where Mr. Andrews could get at them.

Chuck watched closely while Mr. Andrews twisted the band around Chen's leg and tightened it with the pliers.

"It won't hurt him, will it?" Chuck asked anxiously.

"Not a bit," Mr. Andrews answered. "It's very light. He won't even know it's there. And it isn't tight, just snug enough so that it won't bother him by sliding up and down. There, it's done."

He put the pliers in his pocket and turned Chen right side up. *"A-whonk!"* cried Chen miserably, looking at Chuck.

Chuck wanted to tell him he was sorry, that he had

never intended getting either one of them into this situation. But he couldn't. It is hard for a boy to speak to a goose when there are grown-ups standing around watching. Instead, he went up to Chen and put his hand on his back, on those warm rippled brown feathers.

"Watch out for that big bill," Mr. Andrews said. "He can take a real nip out of you if he wants to."

Chuck saw that the game warden had his hand on Chen's long black neck to keep him from doing just that.

"I guess I wouldn't blame him if he did bite me," Chuck said. "If it wasn't for me, he'd be out there with the others."

"I'm going to take him back in just a few minutes," Mr. Andrews told him. "But first there's something I want to show you."

Uncle Bill was looking at Chen. Chuck knew his uncle was wishing Chen and the other geese would stay. And he could see why. Geese were wonderful birds. Now that he knew a little more about them, and had met one personally, he could understand why Uncle Bill was so interested in them.

"Bill," Mr. Andrews began, "I know how hard you've worked to get the geese to winter on the lake, clearing those islands and planting them and all that. Well, you know, I said all along what you needed was some tame geese to decoy the wild ones in and persuade them to stay. And you wouldn't do it."

"It didn't seem fair somehow," Uncle Bill said. "And besides I never could get any geese to use for decoys. You know that."

"Well, watch this!" cried Mr. Andrews.

He raised Chen in his hands and tossed him suddenly into the air. Chen honked twice, flapping his wings frantically. He made an awkward sweeping circle, dropping lower and lower until he crouched in the grass.

Uncle Bill ran and picked him up. "Wing-pulled, by golly," he laughed. "What do you know?"

94

"I figure Chuck must have done it when he was trying to get the goose off the hook this morning," Mr. Andrews went on.

"Oh, I didn't mean to hurt him!" Chuck exclaimed. "I thought you said he was all right."

"He's fine," Mr. Andrews assured him. "He's just lost his primary feathers, so he won't be able to fly for a while. There's no permanent damage done."

Chuck remembered the feathers that had come loose in his hand when he was trying to catch the goose that morning.

"I—I guess I did pull out some feathers," he confessed. "But I didn't know it would keep him from flying."

"Well, it will," chuckled Uncle Bill. "They'll grow again in a few weeks. But in the meantime he'll have to stick around here. And since he's a young goose, his parents will probably stay with him, especially since there's food here and they'll soon learn that it's a safe place."

"And if the parents stay, so will his brothers and sisters, if he has any," Mr. Andrews added. "And if his parents are old and important members of the flock, the whole flock will probably stay. And maybe others will join them. So if they winter here this year, they are likely to come back year after year."

Chuck grinned. Maybe for once, he'd done the right thing, even if he had done it by accident. Maybe he and Chen together had had a wonderful piece of luck.

"Wing-pulled!" repeated Uncle Bill, grinning at Chen. "Say, Jim, take this fellow and get out there with him in a hurry. I don't want the others thinking that he's dead and going off without him."

"Right," said Mr. Andrews. "I'm on my way."

"And Chuck," Uncle Bill went on, "if these geese stay here this winter, I'll—I'll give you my binoculars!"

Chuck stared. "Really, Uncle Bill? Oh, gee, really?"

"It's a promise," Uncle Bill answered, and Chuck grinned. Oh, boy, could he have fun with a pair of binoculars. He could look out his bedroom window and see if Mrs. Smith's mean old boxer was tied up or not, before he took the short cut through her back yard. That was the hatefullest dog for miles around, and Chuck didn't care to meet him if he could help it.

And he could tell if anybody was out playing in the vacant lot. He wouldn't have to walk all the way up there to see. And he could probably see craters on the moon and things like that.

He could even take the glasses to school. Maybe if the other guys wanted to look through them, he'd let them. Johnny Parker and some of his good friends. But mostly he'd do the looking himself, through the wrong end. Maybe arithmetic wouldn't be so bad if you looked at it through the wrong end of a pair of binoculars.

But later as he and Uncle Bill rode back through the woods, Chuck felt sad. He was afraid the geese wouldn't

96

stay. And he wanted them to stay. Even if he wasn't going to get a pair of field glasses, he wanted them to stay. He liked geese. But suppose Chen's mother and father just went off and left him, not caring that he couldn't fly. Or suppose they just stayed long enough for Chen's feathers to grow out again and then went on. Uncle Bill had said it was hard for geese to change their habits. It didn't seem very likely that Chuck would get those glasses.

"How long will it take Chen to grow new feathers?" he asked Uncle Bill as they got out of the jeep.

"Two, maybe three weeks," Uncle Bill answered. "Long enough for the geese to find out this is a good place to winter, I hope."

"How will you know?" asked Chuck.

"Well," said Uncle Bill, "I'll give them a month to make up their minds. I mean to come back out here the day after Thanksgiving. If they're still here then, we can be pretty sure they mean to winter here."

"Can—can I come too?" asked Chuck.

Uncle Bill grinned. "Sure," he said. "Chen wouldn't like it if I came without you. But right now, let's forget about geese. Come along, I'll show you where the wood ducks nested last summer. And maybe we can find one of those fierce voles that kept you awake last night."

When Chuck got back to school, the same old multiplication problem was still on the blackboard. And the teacher said, "Now let me see, I believe Chuck was going to do this problem for us."

And Chuck began, "Six times seven is forty eight . . ." so he knew his luck hadn't really changed. He was just as unlucky as ever, and the geese would never stay. He just about gave up hope right then.

Still, he was counting on going back to the lake with Uncle Bill. They wouldn't spend the night, just drive out to see if they could locate the geese, then eat lunch and drive back.

But even on Thanksgiving Day the old jinx was still working. Chuck woke up with a cold and cough and a fever. Mother let him get up long enough to telephone Uncle Bill and say he couldn't go.

"Are you goig without be?" he asked hoarsely.

"Well, I would have," Uncle Bill answered. "But my old jeep has such a sympathetic nature that when it heard you were sick, right away it developed epizootics of the carburetor, and it'll be a week or so before I can go anywhere. Tell you what, we'll plan to go the first week of Christmas vacation. That's not so far off."

"I thick the geese have left adyway," said Chuck. "Just by luck."

"I don't think I understand that," said Uncle Bill. "But whatever it was, I don't believe it." And he hung up.

As soon as Chuck was well enough to go back to

school, the weather turned bad. It got colder and colder, and late one afternoon it began to snow. Before he went to bed, Chuck called Uncle Bill once again.

"Well, I guess the geese will leave now," he said in a melancholy voice. "I guess it will be too cold for them to stay now."

"Oh, geese don't mind a little cold weather," Uncle Bill replied cheerfully. "As long as the lake doesn't freeze over, they'll be happy. And it will never turn cold enough around here to freeze the lake."

Chuck was surprised. "What do they care about the lake?" he asked. "They don't go swimming in this kind of weather, do they? They'd freeze, wouldn't they?"

"No, they wouldn't," Uncle Bill told him. "Ducks and geese will swim as long as there's an ounce of water for them to swim in, no matter what the temperature is. They don't get cold. They have heavy waterproof feathers on top, and underneath, next to their skins, they have a thick coat of down, the kind of down that's in your comforter, if you're lucky. And under their skins they have a layer of fat that helps keep them warm!"

"Their feet don't have any feathers," Chuck pointed out.

"No, but they have a covering of heavy skin, like big leather boots," Uncle Bill told him. "Besides, geese are used to being out in the weather. If they leave, it won't be on account of the cold."

Chuck was still worried. He had thought birds flew south for the winter so they'd be warm. Before he got into bed he stood by the window, feeling the chill breathing through the glass. Outside, the ground was white with snow and the flakes swirled against the panes. He tried to imagine what it must be like to be a goose, crouching on a sand bar with the sharp wind blowing off the river and the snow piling up all around in a cold black-and-white world.

He ran and jumped into bed. "Mother," he yelled. "Can I have another blanket? I'm freezing!"

Three days later, disaster struck. Only this time, it happened to Uncle Bill.

"I guess I'm so unlucky it rubs off on other people,"

Chuck said gloomily. Uncle Bill looked cross and sat up straighter in his wheel chair.

"I don't think your bad luck had a thing to do with there being an icy patch on the sidewalk in front of Brown's Washateria that I didn't see until I stepped on it," he said. "A broken bone in your foot can happen to anybody."

"Well, anyway, your bad luck is my bad luck," Chuck said with a sigh. "Now we'll never get out there to see if Chen stayed." Suddenly he brightened. "I guess Mr. Andrews will know if Chen is still there. You could call him up and ask him, or write him a letter, couldn't you?"

Uncle Bill gave Chuck a funny look. "Well, the truth is, I did call him," he admitted. "But they've been having

some trouble down the river where the geese spend the winter, and Mr. Andrews was called in to help. He doesn't get back out to our lake more than once a week or so—and he hasn't seen the geese. But that doesn't mean anything. He doesn't have much time to look for them when he's up there.''

Chuck had never felt so downhearted. Even though he had warned himself, he had really believed that Chen was going to stay. He'd counted on it.

"Oh, for Pete's sake, Chuck!" Uncle Bill sounded exasperated. "Don't look so gloomy! If the geese don't stay, it isn't the end of the world. There'll be other winters. And it certainly hasn't anything to do with you and your bad luck!" He frowned at Chuck. "Doesn't anybody in your class ever have bad things happen to them, besides you? Think hard. Don't all your friends get into trouble every now and then?''

Chuck thought hard. "Well, Johnny Parker did shoot his little sister in the stomach with his big brother's BB rifle," he said at last. "But it wasn't his fault. She's got such a fat stomach it just got in the way.''

Chuck thought some more and then went on slowly. "And most of us turn over things and spill things, the boys, I mean. And get stuck in things. Bobby Lawson got stuck in a sewer pipe. And Henry Whitmore hand-cuffed himself to the front door, and it took almost all day to get him loose. And Peter Smith put his blue jeans in the electric drier with a whole lot of bubble gum in the pocket. Boy, was his mother ever mad! She—'' He broke off and looked up at Uncle Bill and grinned. "It just seems worse when it happens to me," he confessed.

It was a long winter for Chuck. Uncle Bill wouldn't even try to find out about the geese. "We'll just go out there some weekend in February and see for ourselves," he told Chuck.

"Well, I sure would like to know what they're doing, that's all," Chuck complained.

"Nothing much," Uncle Bill answered. "They fly a

little and swim a little. They eat corn and grass and what-ever else they can find. But mostly they stand around resting and sleeping and preening their feathers."

"It must be pretty boring," said Chuck.

"Not for them," said Uncle Bill. "It's what they're used to. And not for me either. I can watch them forever. The way they turn their heads and look around, the way they bend their necks or stretch their wings, the way the sun hits the feathers on their backs—everything about them is a wonder to me."

Chuck said nothing. Personally he didn't think he could ever feel that way about a bird, not even Chen. But he couldn't help seeing how badly Uncle Bill would like to get back out to the lake, and he felt sorry for him.

But at last the day arrived. Uncle Bill's foot had healed, the jeep was in good health, and Chuck had about drowned himself in orange juice so he wouldn't have another cold. And he didn't.

The day was gray and frosty. Chuck could see his white breath in the air.

"Do you think they're here?" he asked as he got out of the jeep.

"I've got my fingers crossed," Uncle Bill said. "I'm hoping. As a matter of fact, I can't think why they wouldn't have stayed."

"Well, even if they stayed, maybe something hap-pened to them," Chuck ventured.

"Now there you go," scolded Uncle Bill. "What could happen to them? Nothing much tangles with a full-grown goose, not unless the goose is sick or injured. A fox might try it, but I doubt if he'd get away with it. Or a wild dog—a big dog would stand a better chance. Anyway, it isn't likely that a fox or a dog would be out on those islands."

"You said it was hunters they had to be afraid of," Chuck reminded him.

Uncle Bill made a face at him. "We'll just have to hope all the hunters around here obeyed the law and kept away from the lake," he said.

"Will you get your boat?" asked Chuck hopefully. He was eager to go out in Uncle Bill's boat. "Will you go looking for them in your boat?"

"I may have to," said Uncle Bill. "But I'd rather not. We ought to be able to see them from the shore. If they're here, the chances are they'll be restless."

"Why?" Chuck wanted to know.

"Because it's spring," Uncle Bill answered. "The geese will be flying around, thinking about leaving."

"Spring!" cried Chuck. "It's February. It was twenty-six degrees when we left home!"

"Oh, spring's been here a long time," Uncle Bill told him. "Look, the elder bushes already have little leaves. And see here—" he grabbed a branch as he passed—"the azalea buds are as big as my thumb. I expect you could find a dozen wild flowers in bloom if you looked hard enough. It's spring all right."

"Oh, boy, look, Uncle Bill!" shouted Chuck. "A goose egg!" He ran and picked it up from among the dead leaves, a small white egg.

"Oh, Chuck," said Uncle Bill. "I told you geese didn't nest around here. And I told you their eggs were bigger than hens' eggs. That's hardly as big as a hickory nut."

"Well, I thought it was little because they were just practicing," explained Chuck. "I didn't think any birds would be building a nest in cold weather like this."

"Sure," said Uncle Bill. "Doves, and sometimes robins, for instance. I'm pretty sure this is a dove's egg. Doves start nest-building before they get their Christmas decorations put away." He glanced up into a little pine tree. "There, Chuck, you can see the nest on that crooked limb off to the left there. And the mother dove is sitting on it."

Chuck stared at the scruffy-looking collection of sticks crisscrossed on the branch, and the small-headed, blue-necked brown bird sitting on it. "Doesn't she want this egg?" he asked. "Why did she throw it away?"

Uncle Bill chuckled. "Doves are in such a hurry to build a nest that they don't take much care with it," he said. "They just throw it together any old how, and they often lose eggs through holes in the bottom. This egg is cold. It wouldn't do any good to put it back in the nest. You want to keep it?"

106

Chuck was pleased. He wrapped it in his handkerchief and put it in his jacket pocket. And it must have been three whole minutes before he forgot and rammed his hand in the pocket and squashed the egg. "You'd better not investigate," Uncle Bill told him. "Just throw the whole mess away. If you sneeze, I'll lend you my handkerchief."

"Oh, gee," mourned Chuck. "I was going to try to hatch it myself."

"It wouldn't have worked; I told you the egg was cold," said Uncle Bill, and he grinned. "As a matter of fact, I was just about your age the first time I tried that project myself. And let me warn you, as a mother, a nine-year-old boy is not a howling success."

Chuck grinned too. It would probably have been a lot of trouble. He threw the handkerchief under a bush and they walked on. By and by they came to the spot where they had stood on the famous morning when Chuck caught Chen.

The sun had come out and was gleaming whitely on the water. The sky looked pale and cold. But Uncle Bill was right, Chuck was surprised to find. It was spring. Under the chill there was a warmth and wetness and freshness that was spring.

Far out on the water there were some little dark blobs. Or maybe there weren't. In the glare of the sun it was hard to tell.

"Look there," Uncle Bill said and pointed up. Chuck's mouth gaped open, for the sky was full of long strings and little clouds of birds. They flew high in the air, looking like little black dots, but suddenly one long string circled and descended, landing in the water not too far away.

"Are they geese?" he asked, hardly daring to hope.

Uncle Bill, who was setting up his telescope, shook his head. "No, they're ducks. But I guess the geese will show up soon. You can see how the ducks are stirring around. They feel the spring in the air, and it makes them fidgety."

It was cold sitting there among the bushes, and the ground was hard as iron. Chuck shivered. His legs got cramped and his fingers and toes were numb. It was very dull. He couldn't see anything but the shining water and the bare trees and the little black blobs that Uncle

Bill said were ducks. Chuck couldn't tell. Even when he squinted through the telescope they were only little dark shapes to him. They could have been ducks or geese or driftwood or floating cheeseburgers, as far as he knew.

Every once in a while some of the little dark spots got up off the water and flew around the edge of the lake. And sometimes up from the edge of the sky a new line would appear and Chuck would watch anxiously, hoping that they were geese. He didn't see how Uncle Bill could tell from such a distance. He thought the best thing to do was get the boat and go out there and see whether any of those floating black things were Chen and his family.

Deep in his heart Chuck was ready to give up. Poor Chen. Some fox had caught him while he couldn't fly, or somebody had shot him. It made Chuck furious to think of somebody shooting his goose, his very own big brown bird.

But it must have happened. And all the other geese had flown away from this dreary freezing lake. Uncle Bill was crazy to think geese would stay here. And all these ducks must be crazy, or they would have left too.

Uncle Bill gave Chuck a chocolate bar to eat. It made him feel a little better, but not much. He made it last as long as he could, taking little nibbles first on one side and then on the other. Then it was gone and there was nothing to do again. Time crawled by and Chuck's toes ached with cold. Finally, Uncle Bill spoke.

"I'm afraid you're right, Chuck," he said with a sigh. "The geese must not have stayed. We would surely have seen them by this time—" he broke off. "What's that?" he cried, clutching Chuck's arm. Chuck looked wildly around.

"There, there!" cried Uncle Bill, pointing, and he swung the telescope around.

Then Chuck saw the V of birds coming toward them across the lake. And he knew right away that they were geese. They were much bigger than ducks, and he could see that their wing strokes were slower and deeper and more labored.

The flock was headed straight for the place where Chuck and Uncle Bill were hiding. They came steadily on, flying low and fast. Chuck's heart pounded with excitement. He could see their dark heads and necks. He could see their white throat patches and their dangling feet.

They were right overhead, and now he could hear the sweet singing murmur of their wings!

Suddenly they spoke, crying out to each other in their fierce beautiful voices. The air was filled with the sound of wings and wild things sweeping breathlessly through the sky. A thrill ran over Chuck, his skin prickled, and he almost jumped up to fly with them. He wheeled to watch them go swinging off over the woods as the noise of their voices died slowly away.

For a few minutes he and Uncle Bill stared at each other. Then Chuck drew a deep breath.

"Oh, gosh, oh, gee," he whispered. "They were wonderful, weren't they?"

Uncle Bill nodded. "Look," he said. "They're landing around there on the other side of the lake." And they watched the big birds splash gently into the water.

"Did you notice the second bird on the left as they went over?" asked Uncle Bill. "The big one right behind the leader?"

Chuck shook his head.

"Well, I did," Uncle Bill went on. "He was banded. It must have been Chen."

And he lifted his binoculars over his head and very solemnly hung them around Chuck's neck.